THE RETURN OF THE
RAINBOW GRIEFERS

THE RETURN OF THE RAINBOW GRIEFERS

AN UNOFFICIAL LEAGUE OF GRIEFERS ADVENTURE, #4

Winter Morgan

Sky Pony Press
New York

Copyright © 2015 by Hollan Publishing, Inc.

Minecraft® is a registered trademark of Notch Development AB

The Minecraft game is copyright © Mojang AB

Sky Pony Press books may be purchased in bulk at special discounts for sales promotion, corporate gifts, fund-raising, or educational purposes. Special editions can also be created to specifications. For details, contact the Special Sales Department, Sky Pony Press, 307 West 36th Street, 11th Floor, New York, NY 10018 or info@skyhorsepublishing.com.

Sky Pony® is a registered trademark of Skyhorse Publishing, Inc.®, a Delaware corporation.

Minecraft® is a registered trademark of Notch Development AB.
The Minecraft game is copyright © Mojang AB.

Visit our website at www.skyponypress.com.

10 9 8 7 6 5 4 3 2 1

Library of Congress Cataloging-in-Publication Data is available on file.

Cover photo by Megan Miller

Print ISBN: 978-1-63450-599-4
Ebook ISBN: 978-1-63450-600-7

Printed in Canada

TABLE OF CONTENTS

1
GRAND OPENING

"That was fast!" Noah could hardly catch his breath as he stepped off the Dashing Coaster. The epic, superfast roller coaster was the main attraction at the new amusement park that had opened right outside Violet and Noah's town.

"I want to ride this next," Violet exclaimed as she hurried toward the purple Ferris wheel.

"The Ferris wheel? That's boring. I want something that goes superfast!" Noah loved thrill rides.

The new amusement park was called Supersonic, and people traveled from all around the Overworld for its grand opening. Violet was excited because she helped craft the Tilt-a-Whirl ride. She also had designed the food court for the amusement park. Her good friend Valentino the Butcher owned a restaurant in the food court, and Violet went to visit him. Valentino was serving some customers.

"Can you take a break?" asked Violet.

"Not at the moment," Valentino replied.

"We wondered if you'd like to ride the Dashing Coaster with us," Violet said with a smile.

"I think we've been on it at least ten times. I've lost track," added Noah.

"It sounds like fun, but I have to cook right now." Valentino frowned.

"If you find time for a break, let us know. We'd love to ride the coaster with you." Violet was disappointed Valentino couldn't join them, but she was also eager to explore the rest of the amusement park with Noah.

There were so many rides they hadn't tried out. All the rides used command blocks, so they got to go super-fast and some blocks were able to teleport. Violet pointed to a ride shaped like a large pirate ship, which swayed back and forth. "Let's go on that one!"

Noah agreed and they climbed aboard the pirate ship. When Violet was high up in the air on the ship, right before the ride's severe dip caused her stomach to jump, she saw a flash of pink in the distance. She was very quiet when she stepped off the ride.

"Didn't you like the ride?" asked Noah.

"I did. But I thought I saw something strange when we were on the ship. I think I must have been imagining it." Violet looked off in the distance, but she didn't see anything suspicious. She hoped the pink wasn't from a rainbow griefer's skin; maybe it was just someone walking with colorful cotton candy.

"It's time to go to the opening celebration event," Noah told Violet, and the two headed for the center of the park.

Katie and Leo, the partners who developed the amusement park, stood on a podium and addressed the crowd.

Katie announced, "Welcome to Supersonic. We are all happy to have you here. This park took a lot of planning, but now that it's finished, we want you to enjoy all of the rides!"

The crowd cheered.

Leo stood in front of the log flume. "We are opening the flume now. Line up and be the first to experience this awesome ride!"

Noah and Violet walked to the front of the line. Violet loved the log flume. They sat next to each other, and they both screamed when the flume went down a huge drop with a big splash.

"I think that was my favorite ride," declared Violet when exiting the flume.

"There are so many more rides to go on. I don't think we can pick our favorites yet," replied Noah.

Violet noticed her friends Hannah and Ben walking in the distance and called out to them.

Hannah ran to join them. "Violet and Noah, you have to come with us!"

As Violet and Noah followed Ben and Hannah, Violet asked, "Where are we going?"

Noah didn't like this change in direction. "We went on all the rides in this section of the park already," Noah complained. He was impatient because he wanted to explore the rest of the park.

"We're not going on a ride . . ." Hannah tried to catch her breath.

"We saw something by the Dashing Coaster," Ben told them, "and I think it was a pink—"

Violet interrupted, "Rainbow griefer?"

"Yes!" Hannah was upset.

"I thought I saw a pink rainbow griefer when I was on the roller coaster. I was hoping that I imagined it," Violet exclaimed as she scanned the horizon for the griefer.

"But we disbanded the rainbow griefer army," protested Ben. He didn't understand how they could return. All the rainbow griefers had changed their skins and were living peacefully in the village.

"And we trapped Daniel in the bedrock house. You promised us that he couldn't escape." Hannah looked at Violet as she spoke.

"We have to return to the bedrock house to see if Daniel is still there." Violet headed for the exit.

Kaboom!

"Was that thunder?" Ben stopped and looked up at the dark sky as rain began to fall on the park.

"Zombies!" Hannah shouted.

The amusement park visitors tried to seek shelter from the rain and the zombies. Hordes of people ran toward the food court. Violet, Noah, Hannah, and Ben suited up in diamond armor and charged at the zombies that surrounded Katie and Leo.

"Help us!" Katie called out in terror.

Noah struck a zombie with an arrow. Ben raced toward the zombies with his diamond sword, striking two.

A zombie attacked a villager working at a cotton candy kiosk, transforming him into a zombie villager.

Violet used her diamond sword to destroy the zombie, then she gave the zombie villager a golden apple and splashed a potion on him to save him.

"Thanks!" the villager called to Violet, as she rushed over to help Katie and Leo next.

Katie and Leo tried to fight back, but they didn't have diamond armor. A zombie struck Katie. She was losing energy. With one more hit from the undead beast, she would be destroyed.

Noah hit the zombie that threatened Katie—"Bull's-eye!"

Violet gave Katie some milk to regain her strength.

The sun peeked through the clouds and the zombies disappeared.

"Now I am sure that was a pink rainbow griefer by the Dashing Coaster," Violet exclaimed as she looked at the sky.

"What's a pink griefer?" asked Leo.

Violet described Daniel's griefer army and told Leo and Katie the story about how the gang had helped dissolve the evil army.

"Why do you think this is Daniel's fault?" questioned Katie.

"I have a feeling that zombie attack was staged by Daniel. It's a typical move of his. I'm sure he wants to destroy this amusement park." Violet's mind was racing. She wanted to stop Daniel before he did any damage.

"Why would he want to destroy Supersonic? This is a fun place for everyone in the Overworld." Leo was confused.

"That's exactly why he would destroy it. He doesn't want anyone to have a good time," replied Ben.

"When our village hosted the Olympics, Daniel caused all sorts of trouble. The only way we could stop him was by trapping him in a bedrock house. We need to see if he's still there. I usually go by and check, but I was so busy working on the amusement park, I didn't have time." Violet had many excuses for not visiting Daniel. She disliked traveling outside of town and having to check on him.

"Lead us to Daniel," Katie insisted. "We need to stop him before he stages anymore attacks on Supersonic."

But it was too late. The gang heard someone from the Fun House shout, "Lava!" People poured out of the Fun House as the group rushed toward them.

"What happened?" Violet called to the crowd outside the Fun House.

"Someone flooded the Fun House with lava," a man in a red hat called out.

Leo tried to bring order into the chaotic scene. He told everyone to stay calm and move away from the building. People were still stumbling out of the Fun House as a pool of lava oozed out the front door.

Leo hollered, "Stand back!"

Violet looked at the grassy meadow outside the amusement park. Daniel's bedrock makeshift prison lay just beyond the bucolic landscape. She took a deep breath before heading toward the bedrock home. She wasn't sure what she'd find when she got there.

2

HIDE AND SEEK

Evening approached as Noah, Violet, Hannah, Ben, and Katie made their way to the bedrock house to see if Daniel had escaped.

"Should we turn around?" asked Ben. "It's getting dark."

"No," Violet replied and she took some wood planks from her inventory. "I'll build a shelter quickly."

"Maybe we should go back. I wonder if Leo has gotten the lava situation under control," remarked Katie.

"We'll find out tomorrow. I think it's too dangerous to travel anymore. There are too many hostile mobs at night, and we need to conserve our energy." Violet placed the wooden planks on the ground.

"How can we help you?" asked Hannah.

Violet gave her friend detailed instructions on what she needed to do to help build the house.

The others listened and joined in, and very quickly the house was constructed. The friends each crafted a bed and crawled underneath their wool blankets.

"There is a part of me that hopes Daniel is in the bedrock house, and there is also a part of me that wants him to have escaped," confessed Violet.

"What?" Noah was shocked. "You'd want him to escape?"

"If he didn't escape, that means there is another person who took Daniel's place as the head of the rainbow griefers. I don't want to battle any more people," explained Violet.

"I think I understand you," Noah spoke slowly. "At least we know Daniel, and if he is the one creating all this havoc, we know how to battle him."

"Yes, we do," added Hannah, "but it seems like he's always striking back."

Ben yawned and said, "Daniel is the master of revenge."

"I wonder how he recruited a new army?" Violet pondered, but there was no reply. Everyone had fallen asleep. Violet closed her eyes. She would have her answer in the morning.

At daybreak, the sun shone brightly and cows grazed outside the window. Violet was the first to wake up, and she grabbed some carrots from her inventory and ate them for breakfast.

"Are you up, Violet?" asked Noah.

"Yes," she replied as the others emerged from their beds.

"We have to find Daniel today," Noah stated as he looked out the window. The day had just begun and they had a lot to accomplish.

The gang walked across the field. Violet could spot the bedrock house in the distance.

"I hope Daniel and Mac are still trapped in that house," Violet said as they approached.

Noah hurried toward the small window on the side of the bedrock house. "It looks like someone is in there."

Violet and the gang caught up with Noah. Violet peeked through the window and exclaimed, "That's not a person!"

Daniel had hoped to trick them into thinking he was still in the house. He had left diamond armor on an armor stand in the center of the bedrock room, making it look like the house was still occupied.

Violet opened the door and gasped. "How did he escape?"

Noah inspected the empty bedrock house. "I guess he used pistons to escape."

"I knew we should have kept a guard here." Violet was upset.

Hannah put her arm around Violet. "There was no way we could have found someone who would stay here and guard Daniel. This isn't anyone's fault."

Ben added, "At least we had a short period of peace and harmony in the village."

Everyone agreed that discussing how Daniel had escaped was a waste of time. They needed to come up with a plan for finding this epic trickster.

"Ouch!" Violet screamed.

An arrow had pierced Violet's skin. Within seconds the gang was bombarded with a sea of arrows.

"Looking for me?" Daniel called out, as he stood in front of an enormous army of colorful rainbow griefers. "Fire!" Daniel instructed his army.

The gang wasn't even suited up in diamond armor, so the surprise attack weakened them.

Violet was glad she had some carrots that morning, since she had a bit more energy to fight, but even she was losing hearts. Violet tried to dodge the arrows. She grabbed an arrow from her inventory and shot at the rainbow griefers, but it seemed pointless.

"I can't take any more hits," Hannah called out. She was also trying to battle the griefers with her bow and arrow, but it wasn't working. Two arrows struck Hannah and she was destroyed.

"Oh no!" Ben cried, as he, too, was destroyed.

Katie, Noah, and Violet were the only ones left to battle Daniel and the griefers.

Daniel laughed as Katie was destroyed. "And now I'm left with my two favorite people." Daniel ordered the rainbow griefers to stop shooting arrows.

"What do you want from us?" demanded Violet.

"You thought you were trapping me for life, didn't you?" Daniel laughed again. This time his laugh was quite shrill and piercing in Violet's ears.

"Stop terrorizing us," Noah shouted at Daniel and his new army of rainbow griefers.

"Never," Daniel said with a sinister smile. "It's time for revenge. You guys are going to pay. If you thought I caused a lot of trouble at the Olympic games, wait until you see what I do to your new theme park."

"Leave us alone!" Violet didn't want to beg, but she was exhausted and just wanted Daniel to stop.

Daniel took his diamond sword out of his inventory and walked over to Violet, striking her with his sword. Violet was destroyed. When she awoke in the small cabin, she saw Noah respawning in his bed.

"I guess Daniel destroyed you, too?" she asked.

"Yes," Noah said as he sat up in the bed. "I can't believe how many new soldiers he has working for him."

Ben shook his head. "Me neither. This isn't going to be an easy battle."

"We've beat Daniel in the past, and we can do it again." Hannah was the only one who seemed hopeful.

"I worked so hard to create this amusement park and I'm not going to let Daniel destroy it," said Katie.

There was a knock on the door. The gang suited up in diamond armor before they opened it. They had to be prepared. They didn't know who was on the other side of the door.

3
THE DASHING COASTER

iolet ran to the door. She held her enchanted diamond sword in her hand while she slowly opened the door.

"Katie! Someone has blown up the Dashing Coaster!" Leo stood at the front door.

"What?" Katie was appalled. "I'm sure it was Daniel."

"How's the Fun House doing?" asked Hannah.

"This morning, I went to the amusement park to clean up the Fun House and remove the lava. When I arrived I found the Dashing Coaster was completely destroyed."

"That's awful," said Ben. "We have to go back to Supersonic and help rebuild."

"We also have to come up with a plan to fight Daniel." Violet knew rebuilding was pointless if Daniel was just going to destroy the park again.

A voice boomed from outside the door of the cabin. "Surrender! We have you surrounded."

"It's Daniel!" Violet called out.

"I have a plan. It may seem crazy, but trust me." Noah pulled out some command blocks.

"What are you doing?" asked Violet.

"Don't worry," replied Noah. "It's going to be okay."

They heard a roar in the distance.

"Did you summon the Ender Dragon with command blocks?" Violet questioned Noah with some skepticism.

"Yes, I am using one of Daniel's tricks against him. While Daniel and the rainbow griefers battle the Ender Dragon, we can escape," Noah said, explaining his plan.

The gang heard the rainbow griefers' cries as they attempted to battle the fierce beast that flew through the sky.

"Shoot at it!" Daniel screamed at his army.

The dragon's powerful wings flew by their house and it swooped down, making a hole in the roof.

"We have to leave!" Noah called to his friends.

The gang dashed out of the house and far away from the Ender Dragon.

They didn't look back.

"I see Supersonic!" Violet called out breathlessly.

"Yes, we're almost there!" Ben said happily.

A large crowd milled around in front of the entrance. A woman wearing a park uniform stood on a podium with a megaphone. "The Dashing Coaster is closed today. Please enjoy the rest of the rides at the park. We are open for business."

Some of the crowd stopped by the Dashing Coaster to stare at the rubble. A woman called to the park official, "Is this park safe?"

The park official replied, "We are doing our best to protect all visitors. There is an evil man who wants to destroy this park. But we want to keep it open to prove to him that we aren't afraid."

The crowd roared their support for this plan.

Violet, Noah, and the gang walked into the park. The park official looked at them and told the crowd, "These are the heroes who will save the park."

Violet disliked the attention, though she had to admit it felt nice to have people cheer for her. But she didn't want to be distracted by the attention. She needed to inspect the Dashing Coaster, and she also had to protect the park.

"Wow," Noah exclaimed, looking at the rubble. "Daniel must have used tons of TNT to destroy this coaster."

"I know," Leo replied. "He's a very powerful person, isn't he?"

"Unfortunately, he is," said Violet.

"Oh no!" Hannah called out. "It looks like we have unwelcome visitors."

A host of rainbow griefers stormed through the park's entrance and began striking innocent people with their diamond swords.

"It's war!" Noah shouted.

Folks began to take out their diamond swords and bows and arrows from their inventories and strike back at the rainbow griefers.

Valentino the Butcher shouted to his friends, "Come quick! Someone is trying to blow up the pirate ship ride!"

Violet and Noah broke away from the crowd and rushed toward Valentino. He led them to three blue griefers placing TNT beside the pirate ship.

Noah swiftly took an arrow out of his inventory and shot it at the blue griefers. Violet charged at them and struck one with her diamond sword. Hannah and Ben joined them and shot arrows at the blue griefers, shouting, "Stop!"

"Never!" One of the blue griefers laughed.

Violet used all of her strength to strike the blue griefer as he laughed. She was relieved when he was destroyed. The remaining two blue griefers were horrified.

"We told you to stop," Violet said, confronting them.

"Give us those blocks of TNT," Noah demanded.

The two blue griefers gave up and sprinted away from the gang, leaving the blocks of TNT beside the pirate ride. Bystanders stood and watched as Noah, Violet, Ben, and Hannah picked up the blocks of TNT and placed them in their inventories.

"We need to find out where Daniel has set up his new headquarters," Violet said as she stashed away the final TNT block.

"Yes, and we need to blow it up," suggested Noah.

"Sounds like a plan," agreed Ben.

Cries were heard in the distance. Rainbow griefers were still attacking people in the park.

"We have to help!" Violet headed toward the center of the park, where several griefers were shooting arrows into the crowd.

The people at the park had destroyed most of the griefers and just a few remained. Violet struck a weakened griefer and destroyed him. Noah, Ben, and Hannah hit the last few griefers. The park was now temporarily free of rainbow griefers, but the gang knew that wouldn't last. They had to secure the park.

A park official roamed around Supersonic announcing that the park was still open. Despite their exhaustion from the battle with the rainbow griefers, park attendees lined up to go on the many exciting rides. Young and old ate cotton candy and tried to enjoy the remaining hours of sunlight.

Leo jogged up to the gang and announced, "I know how Daniel is getting the soldiers for his army!"

4

NEW RECRUITS

"**H**ow is he getting them?" Violet asked.

"I captured a griefer," Leo told them. "I have him trapped in my office."

The gang followed Leo to his office to meet with the imprisoned rainbow griefer.

"I hope he's still there," remarked Hannah.

"I'm sure he is," Leo said confidently.

They reached the small office near the rubble from the Dashing Coaster. Leo opened the door. A green griefer stood in his office, looking troubled.

"I want to change my skin," confessed the green griefer.

"Okay," replied Leo, "if you think that will make you feel better."

"I don't want to be a griefer for one more minute. I despise it. I never wanted to be an evil rainbow griefer, but Daniel forced me."

"How?" asked Violet.

"First, we should let him change," interrupted Leo. "It obviously bothers him to wear the green skin." Leo looked at the green griefer with some sympathy.

The green griefer chose a skin with black pants, a tan shirt, and a red hat. "Thank you for letting me change. Daniel has taken over my town. I live in a desert village and Daniel has been terrorizing us. He threatened the town with daily attacks from the Wither and the Ender Dragon, and he flooded most of our homes with lava or blew them up with TNT."

"That sounds just like Daniel," concurred Noah.

"He told us if we didn't change our skins to rainbow skins, he would put us all on Hardcore mode. One by one, each resident of the town began to choose different color skins and change into rainbow griefers. He also made us change our names. We were only called by our colors. My griefer name was Greengriefer81."

"What's your real name?" asked Hannah.

"Marco," he replied.

"Well, you're safe now Marco. But we need you to help us. You must tell us more about Daniel's invasion tactics," said Violet.

Marco was happy to tell them all the details of Daniel's invasion of his desert village. "After he took over, Daniel began to give us various tasks. Most of them were focused on destroying this amusement park."

"What does he have planned?" questioned Ben.

"I was a part of the attack today. I know he is planning a lot of other stuff, but he doesn't let us know everything. If you want me to, I can lead you to my town.

Daniel is living there in an old desert temple that he looted."

"Yes, we want to go there," said Violet.

"Someone has to stay here," Katie remarked as she looked at Violet. "You can't leave me alone to defend this park. I worked too hard developing it to have it destroyed."

"I'll stay here and help you," offered Ben.

"Me, too," added Hannah.

"I think Noah and I can go alone with Marco," Violet offered. She paused to think and then suggested, "Maybe we should change into rainbow skins when we get closer to your village. That way we can blend in."

"I never want to wear a rainbow skin again," protested Marco.

"I know how you feel, but that might be our only way to surprise Daniel. I don't want to wear a rainbow griefer skin either," Noah said, trying to reason with Marco.

"How far is your town? I'm not familiar with the Desert Biome," Violet asked as she looked at the evening sky. "It's getting dark. We have to get going."

Violet walked out of the office. Folks were hurrying around the park.

Noah followed Violet and observed, "Something isn't right here. I think Daniel is about to stage another attack."

Valentino the Butcher ran up to them. "The Wither!" he said breathlessly. "Look!"

The gang looked up at the sky. The Wither was flying around the park's entrance shooting wither skulls at the people standing by the ticket booth.

"I have snowballs!" Violet called out as she raced toward the Wither and threw a snowball at the three-headed beast.

"Oh no!" Hannah cried out as a roar boomed throughout the amusement park. "Daniel has also summoned the Ender Dragon."

Daniel wasn't there to watch his evil plan backfire. Instead of the Ender Dragon and the Wither attacking the people at the park, the two hostile beasts began to battle each other.

"Wow, this is intense!" Noah said as he watched the battle in the sky. The Wither shot skulls at the Ender Dragon as the winged creature flew at the Wither, striking it with its powerful body. The Ender Dragon and the Wither began losing energy. The crowd watched while trying to shelter themselves from the wither skulls flying through the air.

"Run to safety," a park official encouraged the crowd.

People began to exit the park as the Ender Dragon swooped by the log flume, almost crushing the ride with a strike from its wing. The Wither began to fade and, within seconds, it exploded. Violet ran toward the weakened dragon and threw snowballs at the monster. Noah shot arrows. Violet was happy when she destroyed the Ender Dragon with the last snowball from her inventory.

"It's almost nighttime," Noah reminded them as he looked at the sky.

"We should leave for the desert in the morning," Violet told Marco. "You can stay with us at our tree house tonight. The whole gang will be staying with us, too."

Marco was excited. "Wow! I've never slept in a tree house before. What fun!"

The gang left the park as the sky grew darker.

Two Endermen walked by. The gang tried to avoid looking them in the eyes, yet one of the Endermen shrieked and teleported next to Marco. Violet struck the Enderman with her diamond sword, but the Enderman was very powerful.

"I have a plan!" Noah shouted to them. "Follow me!"

The gang followed Noah to the shore as he jumped into the deep blue water. The two Endermen also dove into the water, and they were destroyed.

Noah swam back to the shore and pointed fondly at the tree house. "Look, we are home."

They climbed the ladder to the tree house and when they entered the living room, they were shocked to see a stranger standing by their fireplace.

5
REMEMBER ME?

"**W**ho are you?" asked Violet.

Noah took out his diamond sword and warned the stranger, "Get out of here." He held the sword to the stranger's chest.

"Please, don't hurt me," the stranger pleaded.

"Tell us who you are!" Violet said angrily.

"I'm a friend of Trent's. He's in trouble and he asked me to find you." The stranger stuttered, "My n-name is W-Will. I'm a treasure hunter. Your friend Trent is being trapped by an evil griefer named Mac."

"Where is he?" asked Violet.

"He's in the jungle. We were unearthing treasure from a jungle temple when Mac captured Trent. My friends Max, Lucy, and Henry tried to save him, but Mac trapped them, too. I barely escaped. I was lucky to have a potion of invisibility and I splashed it on myself to get away. I only had enough for me. I felt bad about using it, but Trent told me that I should escape and come here and find you. He said you'd help him. He said you know all about Mac." Will was so anxious that he almost said this in one breath.

"We have to help Trent." Violet looked over at Noah.

Marco was surprised at this change in plans. "Trent? We need to go to my desert village and stop Daniel. He is turning my entire village into evil rainbow griefers."

Ben and Hannah spoke quietly to each other, then Ben said, "We must go save Trent."

Katie asked, "I thought you were helping us? I thought you guys were staying here. We can't let Supersonic get destroyed."

Violet paced around the living room; she wasn't sure what she should do. She wanted to help everyone, but that wasn't possible. "We can't let our friend Trent get destroyed by Mac. This is a hard choice. I'm not sure what to do."

"Maybe we can go find Trent and then head to the desert village. Once we save him, he can help us. And I'm sure Mac is working with Daniel," stated Hannah.

"But who is going to stay here and help us save the park?" asked Katie.

Kaboom!

"What was that?" Noah was terrified.

Everyone rushed to the large window. Smoke rose from Supersonic.

"I hope Daniel didn't destroy the park!" Leo was horrified.

"We have to see what damage he caused," Katie said and she started down the ladder.

"Stop!" shouted Violet. "That's what Daniel wants us to do. It's probably a trap."

"I can't just sit here while Supersonic burns to the ground!" Katie was furious and frustrated.

"Violet's right," Ben said calmly, "heading to Supersonic in the middle of the night isn't going to help us."

"Let's just all get some sleep here, so we can respawn in the tree house if we get destroyed." Violet tried to sound practical.

There was a rustling on the ladder.

"What's that?" asked Hannah.

Noah ran to the ladder and shouted, "It's spiders."

"That's not such a big deal," Violet shrugged. "Just shoot arrows at them."

"There are hundreds of them!" exclaimed Noah, as he looked at the endless pairs of piercing red eyes staring at him.

The gang crowded the small entrance by the ladder and shot arrows at the spiders. Violet used her diamond sword to strike any spiders that made their way into the tree house.

"This has to be Daniel's work!" Ben said as he shot an arrow at the never-ending parade of arachnoids that crept up the ladder.

Hannah grabbed a splash potion and threw it at the spiders on the ladder, destroying all of them.

Noah placed his bow and arrow in his inventory. He then put on diamond armor, grabbed his enchanted diamond sword, and climbed down the ladder.

"What are you doing?" asked Violet.

"I need to find the spawner. It can't be very far from here," Noah called to them as he climbed onto the ground and struck a spider with his sword. He found the spawner underneath the house. Noah looked up and saw Violet standing by him holding a torch.

"I couldn't let you do this alone," Violet said, and she placed the torch by the spawner.

Noah and Violet deactivated the spawner and climbed up the ladder to the tree house.

"We have to get some sleep." Violet smiled at her friends, climbed into bed, and crawled underneath the wool covers.

Kaboom! Another explosion was heard in the distance.

"I can't sleep knowing Daniel is blowing up the amusement park," Katie cried.

"I know how you feel. I worked on the park, too," Violet comforted her. "But sleeping is our only option. We need our energy and we also need to have the same respawning point. Both will work to our advantage."

As the gang drifted off to sleep, Violet wondered if there would be anything left of Supersonic in the morning. She also knew that she had to help Trent. There was so much to do. As she tried to close her eyes, she spotted a pair of red eyes looking up at her. She quickly grabbed her diamond sword from her inventory and pounded the spider crawling across the tree house floor. Violet inspected the rest of the floor. When she saw it was empty, she climbed back into bed and fell asleep.

Kaboom! Another explosion broke the silence, but nobody woke up. They were all asleep, dreaming of defeating Daniel.

6
CHOICES

Violet woke up and went to the large window. "I don't see any more smoke coming from Supersonic."

Katie rushed to Violet's side. "I can still see the Ferris wheel! Maybe the entire park isn't destroyed!"

"We have to go investigate," Leo said as he walked toward the ladder.

"Yes, but we all have to eat first." Violet handed everyone milk and cake. They devoured the morning treats and their energy bars were restored.

"Before we head our separate ways, I think we should all stop by the park," Noah told the gang.

Everyone agreed. The group made their way to Supersonic. Despite the explosions the night before, folks were lined up to get inside the amusement park.

"We have a delayed opening today," the park official announced.

Katie and Leo rushed to find out what had happened. Katie asked, "What was blown up last night? We could heard the explosion, but we weren't able to see what was destroyed."

The park official listed several rides that had been blown up. "Even the Tilt-a-Whirl is gone," she said sadly.

"That's okay. We will rebuild all the rides and have a grand reopening. But now we have to focus on stopping the attacks," Katie told the official, explaining that she and Leo would stay behind to guard the park.

"Hannah and I can stay behind with you," added Ben.

"No, you should go with Marco. They'll need all the help they can get," Leo told him.

They said their goodbyes as Violet, Noah, Hannah, Ben, Marco, and Will left the village and headed into the expansive Overworld.

Will said, "I can lead you to Trent and Mac. I have a map."

Marco added, "And I can lead you to the desert village."

"I think we should release Trent first. He will help us defeat Daniel." Violet worried whether she had made the right choice, but she was certain that Trent would be able to help them defeat Daniel.

The gang agreed with Violet. They had to find Trent in the jungle temple. Will looked at the map and led the gang through a Grassy Biome until they reached the Swamp Biome. A bat flew overhead.

"The swamp is the worst. I hate slimes and witches," Hannah groaned.

"Nobody likes slimes and witches," added Ben.

As the gang made their way deeper into the swamp, walking along a pond of murky water covered with lily pads, they spotted a witch's hut.

"I hope that hut is empty," Hannah said as she took out a potion and her sword. She wanted to be prepared.

"Me too." Violet didn't want to fight a witch—she wanted to find Trent in the jungle and then head to the desert to stop Daniel.

"It's not empty!" Marco called out.

A purple-robed witch emerged from the hut, clutching a potion bottle in one hand.

Noah rushed toward the witch and struck her with his diamond sword. Violet shot an arrow at her. Hannah lunged at the witch with her sword, but the witch threw a potion of harming on Hannah.

"She got me!" Hannah cried out.

Noah struck the witch again, but she was able to splash a potion on him, too.

"I've been hit, too!" Noah called to Hannah.

Marco raced to Noah and Hannah and handed them milk to drink.

Violet struck the witch with her diamond sword and destroyed her. The witch dropped a spider's eye, which Violet quickly picked up and placed in her inventory.

"Everyone okay?" asked Violet.

"Yes," Hannah replied after finishing the milk.

"We need to get out of the swamp," exclaimed Ben.

Will studied the map. "It's not that far to the jungle. We won't be in the swamp much longer."

Boing! Boing! Boing!

"Slimes!" shouted Hannah. "Seriously? This is the worst trip to the swamp ever!"

"At least it's not too dark or we'd have even more hostile mobs to battle," said Noah. He tried to look on the bright side, but it was hard to be cheerful—a trip to the swamp wasn't fun at all.

Noah struck one of the slimes with his diamond sword and told everyone to destroy the smaller slimes. "I can get the large slimes, but we have to obliterate the smaller ones or we'll never get out of here."

Hannah hit one of the small slimes and destroyed it. "I got one!"

"Don't get too excited," Violet cautioned. "I see a bunch of slimes bouncing toward us."

"And I see another witch!" Marco called out.

Marco and Will battled the witch, avoiding splashes from her potions, while the others fought the slimes. The sun was setting as the gang finished their battle with the swamp creatures.

"We need to get out of here," Will said as he studied the map. "There is a Grassy Biome right outside the jungle. We can build a shelter there and find Trent in the morning."

The gang hurried out of the swamp before the sun set. Soon the full moon would shine over the swamp biome. The gang reached an open patch of land. Cows were grazing in the distance.

"I have enough wood. Just help me build a house," said Violet.

The group helped Violet construct a house, and they all crafted beds. The sun was setting. They each climbed into their beds and fell asleep. This time there were no explosions keeping them up. They were sleeping peacefully, until someone walked in the door.

7
NOT THE NETHER

"**W**ake up!" Daniel screamed.

Violet thought she was having a nightmare. She opened her eyes and Daniel was standing in the middle of their crudely constructed cabin. He had at least a dozen rainbow griefers with him and they were all pointing their swords at the gang.

"What do you want? You've pretty much destroyed the amusement park. Aren't you done torturing us?" Violet shouted at Daniel and his evil griefers.

"Done?" Daniel laughed, "I've just begun."

Hannah carefully took out a potion from her inventory and splashed it on Daniel.

"Ugh!" Daniel shouted.

"Quick!" Hannah called to the others. They jumped out of their beds, and while Hannah splashed potions on the griefers, the gang was able to escape.

"We're safe!" Marco called out as they entered the jungle.

"No, we're not," Noah said.

Arrows flew through the air. One struck Hannah. Everyone looked for rainbow griefers, but there were none in sight.

"Who is shooting arrows at us?" Violet couldn't see anyone, but she could feel the arrows pierce her skin.

"Skeletons!" Noah shouted.

Click! Clack! Clang! A group of bony monsters ambled toward the group, aiming their arrows at the gang.

"I don't think I have enough energy to fight them," Violet said. Her energy bar was very low. She had been hit too many times.

"Me neither," said Ben. His health bar was almost drained.

Hannah looked through her inventory. She wanted to give everyone a potion to help them regain their strength. "I don't have any potions left!"

"I have a plan," Noah said as he shielded himself from the barrage of arrows heading in their direction.

"What?" Violet questioned. She had no idea how they could stop the skeleton attack. She looked at Noah. "Are you building a portal?"

"Yes," he said as he placed the blocks of obsidian on the ground and a purple mist rose from the portal.

"Not the Nether!" Marco was frightened. He had never been to the Nether.

"It's the only way we can survive." Noah hopped on the portal. "Join me!"

The gang gathered close to Noah. In an instant, they reemerged in the deep red Nether.

"Watch out!" Noah called to Violet. "There's a pool of lava behind you."

"I don't understand why you thought this was a good idea." Violet was annoyed. "There are way too many hostile mobs down here. We're all going to be destroyed."

Will took some carrots out of his inventory. "We should eat something to regain our energy."

The gang ate the carrots as they made their way through the lava-filled Nether.

Soon Violet spotted a Nether fortress. "Look! Maybe we can find treasure in there."

"I need Nether wart for my potions," Hannah said and she rushed to the fortress.

"Don't run," Noah warned. "We need to conserve our energy."

The group walked toward the fortress. When they reached the entrance Violet said, "I can't believe we haven't seen any hostile mobs yet. This is terrific. What a great idea, Noah."

Hannah stopped by a patch of soul sand by the stairs and began to pick Nether wart.

Will led them toward the treasure. He was confident that he'd find a chest. "I've gotten treasure from many Nether fortresses."

The gang followed closely behind Will, but stopped when they saw a large pool of lava.

"Watch out," Will said as a blaze swam through the lava. The yellow blaze stared at them with its menacing black eyes and began to shoot three fireballs at Violet and Noah.

Luckily they were able to dodge the fireballs, but within seconds, the blaze shot another three fireballs at Marco and Will.

Marco surprised everyone when he unearthed a snowball from his inventory and threw it at the blaze, obliterating it.

"We need to be careful," Will warned as he inspected the pool of lava. "A lot of Nether fortresses have blaze spawners. We must make sure we're prepared for another attack."

"Aren't they usually found in the outdoor rooms?" asked Violet.

"Yes," replied Will. "So let's stay indoors and find the treasure." Will led them to a room with a chest. He slowly walked over to the chest. "I have to make sure it isn't booby-trapped."

"I wonder what's inside." Marco was excited. Although he was scared of being in the Nether, he had to admit he was also secretly thrilled. This was the first time he was opening treasure in a Nether fortress.

Will opened the chest and found it filled with blue diamonds. "Diamonds!" he called out.

"Wow!" Marco looked inside the chest and picked up a diamond, placing it in his inventory.

"There are enough diamonds for everyone," Will said. He handed diamonds to everyone in the group.

Violet took the last diamond and carefully placed it in her inventory. Suddenly she saw a dark block hop into the small room.

"Magma cubes!" Will called out.

Noah struck the magma cube with his sword, but the hit didn't destroy the magma cube, it just created smaller cubes.

"This is just like fighting a slime," Ben gasped as he struck one of the smaller cubes with his sword.

"We don't really have the energy to fight these cubes," Violet warned as she looked at her health bar, which was slowly decreasing. She struck a magma cube that pounced at her.

"I can't fight either," added Ben.

"We need to get back to the Overworld. We have the Nether wart and the diamonds. Do we have enough obsidian to make a portal?" questioned Hannah.

"Yes, just help me fight the magma cubes," Noah replied and he struck another cube.

The group used diamond swords and bows and arrows to destroy the cubes.

Will instructed, "Don't worry about the smaller cubes. They aren't that dangerous. As long as we stand on a block, they can't hurt us."

When the final cube was destroyed, the gang hurried out of the fortress.

While Noah crafted a portal back to the Overworld, he joked, "That trip was short but sweet."

"Sweet?" Violet disagreed. "You're not funny."

Noah's portal was complete. The group stood on the platform and a purple mist rose out of the ground as they returned to the Overworld.

8

BACK IN THE OVERWORLD

The sun was setting when they reached the Overworld. Violet looked around, but she wasn't sure where they were.

"I think I see Supersonic," Ben said in surprise.

"Yes, I see the Ferris wheel," confirmed Violet.

"We ended up where we started." Ben was annoyed.

"What's up, Noah?" Hannah frowned at her friend.

"Don't blame me. I wasn't sure where we'd reemerge. Also I saved us from the skeleton attack. If the skeletons had destroyed us, I'm sure Daniel and his griefers would have been waiting for us in that house. They would have annihilated us."

"Noah's right. This isn't his fault. We need to go back to the tree house and get some rest. Tomorrow we will go find Trent." Violet started toward the tree house.

The group climbed up the ladder to the tree house, and they were surprised to see Trent standing in the living room.

"Trent!" Violet called out. "We were about to rescue you."

"Will," Trent said. He was very happy to see his friend. "I'm glad you were able to find my friends."

"How did you escape?" asked Noah.

"It wasn't easy, but three treasure hunters—Henry, Lucy, and Max—helped me. They threw a potion on Mac and then we all attacked him with whatever weapons we had and he was destroyed." Trent paced as he spoke.

"I bet he's going to come looking for you," warned Noah.

"I'm not worried. We can defeat him." Trent was confident of his friend's skills. They were warriors.

"I guess I don't have to stick around," Will said as he looked out at the dark sky, "but can I stay here for the night? I don't want to get destroyed by hostile mobs."

"Yes, you can stay here tonight," Violet told him, "and you don't have to leave. If you want to help us defeat Daniel and rebuild the amusement park, we would love your help."

"You guys have been so nice to me. I think I'll stay until you defeat Daniel. And I want to be the first one to ride the famed Dashing Coaster when it's rebuilt." Will was surprised to realize how happy he was that they had asked him to stay. He was a treasure hunter who was always exploring the Overworld, but he liked having a place that felt like a home—a place where people cared about him, and where he wanted to help others.

"We should get into bed. It's the only way we can be safe," Violet told them. Everyone crawled into their beds and fell asleep.

The morning wasn't very peaceful. Within minutes of waking up, there was a loud explosion.

"I bet the park is completely gone now," Hannah said with dismay. She didn't want to look out the window.

Noah walked to the window. "No, it's not the park. It looks like smoke is coming from the village."

The gang hurried down the ladder of the tree house. When they reached the center of the village, they saw a large hole in the ground. The iron golem was missing as well as a bunch of shops.

"Valentino," Noah called to his friend Valentino the Butcher. "What happened?"

"Two red griefers sprinted into the center of town and left blocks of TNT. It was awful. I'm glad nobody was hurt."

"I knew you'd show up!" a voice boomed from behind them. It was Daniel. Mac stood next to him, and there was a large griefer army behind them.

Noah shouted, "Rainbow griefers! You don't have to listen to Daniel. We want to save you."

"Save them?" Daniel laughed. "They don't need to be saved. They *want* to be here."

Mac aimed his bow and arrow at Trent. The arrow pierced Trent's arm.

Noah grabbed his diamond sword and rushed toward Mac. "Leave us alone!"

Trent gathered his energy and removed a bow and arrow from his inventory and hit Mac.

The army of rainbow griefers descended upon the group. It was a full-on battle. The gang used up all the weapons and potions in their inventories, but they were still losing the battle.

"This isn't going to work," Violet whispered to Noah as they fought side by side.

"Yes, it is!" Noah's eyes grew wide and he grinned.

"What?" Violet was confused until she saw townspeople wearing diamond armor running in their direction.

The townspeople outnumbered the griefers and the army was rapidly diminishing.

"We're winning!" Hannah called out.

"There's no winning and losing here. We are just surviving," Violet added as she struck two orange griefers with her enchanted diamond sword.

The battle was long and everyone was exhausted. There were only a couple of rainbow griefers left, and soon they were all destroyed.

"We did it!" Ben called out.

"Where's Daniel?" asked Noah.

"Where's Mac?" asked Violet.

There was no answer.

"Did somebody destroy them?" questioned Will.

Nobody had destroyed Daniel or Mac.

"That means they must be nearby," concluded Violet.

"It also means they must be planning something." Noah looked around to see where Daniel and Mac were hiding, but he saw no clues to their whereabouts.

"We need to head to my desert village," Marco reminded them, "that's the best way to stop him."

"It's the only way," clarified Violet. "Daniel will be weak when his army is destroyed. We were able to destroy him before, and we *will* do it again."

Katie and Leo joined the gang. Katie said, "Someone flooded the park with lava. We can't even go inside."

"That's awful!" Violet was devastated; she had worked very hard on the park.

"We are going to start rebuilding," said Leo.

"We will help you rebuild," Noah said quite confidently, "but first we must go to the desert."

Together the gang left the town and headed in the direction of the Sandy Biome.

9
ALMOST THERE

The Savanna Biome was on the outskirts of the Desert Biome. The gang trekked through dry grass as horses grazed around the land.

"I see a village," Violet pointed out.

"Do you know anyone from this village?" Noah asked Marco.

"No, I don't," Marco confessed. "I rarely left the Desert Biome."

"We should trade some diamonds for food and other resources," suggested Ben.

The village was rather small. There were only a few shops on the main street. Noah stopped in front of the blacksmith's shop. "Should we get more armor?"

"I need to trade my diamonds for a diamond chestplate," Marco told them.

They entered the shop. Marco asked the blacksmith if he had a diamond chestplate.

The blacksmith greeted them warmly. "It's so nice to finally see someone walk through the door who isn't wearing a rainbow skin."

Violet gasped, "Are most of the people in this village wearing rainbow skins?"

The blacksmith nodded his head and replied, "They are coming from the desert village not far from here. But I think some people in this town are beginning to change their skins to rainbow skins."

"Why?" asked Violet.

The blacksmith paused, "I'm not sure. But I can tell you that business has never been better. It's as if this entire town and the desert village is preparing for an incredible battle. I am running low on armor and swords. You're lucky I have this diamond chestplate left in stock."

Marco traded his diamonds and thanked the blacksmith for the chestplate.

"We must head to the desert village now," Marco told the man.

"I'm not sure they'll let you in the village. They have guards stationed outside the entrance to the town," the blacksmith replied.

"Guards?" Marco was horrified. His village used to be so peaceful.

"Why?" questioned Noah.

"I don't know why they have guards, but I assume they don't want strangers entering the town," said the blacksmith.

"I'm not a stranger. The Desert Biome is my home," Marco told the blacksmith.

"Then I'm sure they'll let you in," the blacksmith replied with a smile.

The gang walked through the small savanna village and toward the Desert Biome. As the grass turned to sand, they spotted the rainbow guards stationed by a makeshift checkpoint outside of town.

"We need to hide," Violet instructed the group, as she snuck behind a building.

"I think we should change into rainbow skins," advised Noah. He didn't want to do this, but he knew it was a good strategy.

"I can't do it," Marco replied defiantly.

"If we are going to get into that town and destroy Daniel, you need to pick a rainbow skin," coaxed Noah.

"You should use your old skin," suggested Hannah.

Everyone was surprised to see that Violet was the first to put on a pink skin. "I actually think I look good."

"Your name is Violet. I assumed you would have picked purple," Trent joked.

"I like pink," Violet replied with a smile.

"Don't have too much fun as a pink griefer," Noah told Violet as he put on an orange skin.

Marco was the last person to put on a skin. He went back to his original green skin.

Violet took a deep breath as they approached the checkpoint.

"Who are you?" the red griefer standing guard at the checkpoint asked them.

"I'm Greengriefer81." Marco was shaking.

"Okay," the red griefer said, "you can go."

The others followed Marco, but the guard said, "Stop. I didn't say you could all go. I just said he could enter the town."

"I'm Pinkgriefer55," Violet blurted out.

The guard paused. Violet's heart skipped a beat.

"I'm sorry, but can you repeat your name?" The guard stared at Violet.

"Pinkgriefer55," she replied slowly.

"We don't use numbers under sixty. Are you sure you didn't forget your number?" the red griefer questioned.

"Yes!" Violet smiled. "I meant Pinkgriefer65."

"That's better," said the red griefer. "You can go ahead. But make sure you remember your number. I also had a hard time remembering mine at first. One day I was Joe, and the next day I'm Redgriefer89."

"Joe?" Marco stood next to Violet. "Were you a cactus farmer?"

"Yes, I am. I mean I was. Who are you?" The red griefer was surprised that anyone knew him.

"I am Marco." Marco hastily corrected himself, "I mean—I was Marco. Now I am Greengriefer81."

"Marco!" The red griefer exclaimed, "Er . . . Greengriefer81, it's so nice to see you again. I remember you lived down the road from me."

"I miss those days." Marco immediately regretted saying those words. He was afraid the red griefer would get mad at him. Daniel was in charge now and the griefer had to respect him. Marco knew if they didn't play along, they wouldn't be able to overthrow Daniel.

Everyone was shocked when the red griefer said, "I miss my farm."

Marco wanted to tell Joe the red griefer how they planned to take over the desert village, and how Joe would be able to produce cacti again, but he knew that wasn't a good idea. He wasn't sure he could trust Joe.

The gang entered the desert village. Noah pointed to a desert temple. "Is that where Daniel has his headquarters?" he asked Marco.

"Yes, that's it." Marco stared at the desert temple. "How are we ever going to get inside that temple and overthrow Daniel? It seems impossible."

"We need a good plan," Violet said, as various ideas raced through her head.

Before they could come up with a plan, an arrow struck Hannah's unarmored yellow skin.

"Ouch," she called out.

"Stop!" Joe shouted. A group of a dozen rainbow griefers stood by him. "They are traitors!"

The gang ran as they tried to dodge the arrows that flew in their direction.

"How are we going to escape?" Ben questioned.

"We're not!" Noah replied as he headed toward the desert temple, and the others followed closely behind.

10
STRUGGLE IN THE SAND

"This way!" Noah directed the others as they stormed the desert temple.

"Intruders!" screamed a blue and red griefer stationed by the door.

"But they're rainbow," cried a red and white griefer. "They're like us! We are being attacked by our own people!"

"Don't be fooled by their rainbow skins. They are in disguise," Joe called out when he reached the desert temple. He shot arrows at the gang as they made their way into the temple.

Noah and Violet ducked to avoid strikes from the numerous arrows flying at them.

"We have to fight hard!" Ben shouted to his friends, and he struck two rainbow griefers with his sword.

"Yes, there's no time to think," Hannah replied. She was using all of her energy simply striking the rainbow griefers that surrounded her.

Noah, Violet, Marco, Trent, and Will were battling Joe and his small group of colorful creeps, when they heard a loud voice boom throughout the desert temple.

"Welcome to my home!" Daniel laughed.

The gang was shocked when Daniel and Mac appeared before them. The armor-clad villains held a diamond sword and a bottle of potion. Daniel splashed a potion on Violet, Will, Marco, and Trent.

Noah dodged the splash and struck Daniel's arm with his diamond sword.

Hannah also escaped the potent potion that weakened Violet and the others. She threw a splash potion on Mac and Daniel.

Violet's energy returned quickly. She joined Hannah and struck Daniel with her sword. *This is too easy*, she thought.

Violet worried that this was a staged attack. She wondered if Daniel and Mac wanted to be destroyed so they would respawn someplace where they could plan an even more sinister attack. Violet stopped hitting Mac and Daniel with her sword.

"What are you doing?" Daniel was confused. "Don't you want to destroy me?"

"Yes, but this just doesn't feel right." Violet couldn't believe she said those words.

"What are you talking about?" Noah asked. He didn't understand why Violet was giving up.

Mac's diamond sword pierced Violet's leg.

"Ouch!" she called out.

The sun began to set. "Now you won't have to fight only us, you'll have to battle the hostile mobs too!" Daniel laughed.

"Unless we destroy you first." Mac struck Violet again.

Noah, Trent, and Will used all of their energy and destroyed Daniel and Mac. Violet just stood and watched. She couldn't help but wonder why Daniel and Mac would let themselves be exposed. They had an army to protect them. Why would they bother risking a battle?

Violet got her answer when she saw Daniel and Mac storm through the desert temple with a new batch of fully energized rainbow griefers. She realized that the desert temple wasn't Daniel's headquarters. He must sleep somewhere else.

"Get them!" Daniel ordered his band of rainbow griefers.

Those were the last words Violet remembered. Within seconds she had respawned in the tree house in her pink rainbow skin. She changed back into her old skin. There was no point in remaining pink when Daniel already knew what she looked like in disguise.

Violet looked around for the others, but nobody else had respawned. It was nighttime. She peered out the window. Violet wanted to head back to the desert and help her friends, but she knew it was much too dangerous to travel at night, especially when she was alone.

A pair of red eyes stared back at her.

"A spider!" Violet called out, but there was nobody there to hear or help her. She struck the spider with her diamond sword and crawled back into bed. She knew it was important to get some rest.

As Violet pulled the blue wool blanket over her body and closed her eyes, she caught a glimpse of Noah respawning on his bed.

"Noah?" Violet got out of her bed. "Are you okay?"

A groggy Noah looked at his friend. "You're right. Daniel was staging something else. He wanted us to destroy him so he could respawn in the other location. The new batch of rainbow griefers was ruthless."

"How? Didn't they destroy the others?"

"They have taken everyone prisoner. They accidentally destroyed me," replied Noah. "Wait, Violet . . . you're not pink anymore?"

"No, and you should change back to your old skin too," suggested Violet.

Noah changed his skin. "I feel so much better now."

Violet was concerned with the fate of their friends. "What are they planning on doing to the others?"

"I'm not sure, but we have to save them," Noah said. He got up from the bed, grabbed some potatoes from his inventory, and began to eat one. He offered a potato to Violet and she thanked him.

Violet took a bite of the potato. She wanted to be strong so she could save her friends.

As they sat on their beds and ate, they heard someone on the ladder.

"Who's there?" Violet was nervous.

"It's Katie and Leo," Katie called out.

Leo sounded exhausted when he said, "Someone blew up our home with TNT. We barely escaped."

Violet gave food to her weary friends and then said, "I think we should all sleep here. In the morning you can come with us to the desert. We have to stop Daniel and Mac. They have trapped our friends."

"Tomorrow?" Noah seemed upset. "We have to go now. There isn't a minute to lose."

"We can't travel at night. It's too dangerous," replied Violet.

"I am afraid that by morning our friends might be destroyed." Noah's voice shook as he said these words.

"We will go with you," Leo told Noah. "We can travel at night. We're not afraid of hostile mobs."

Violet reluctantly agreed to go and the gang climbed down the ladder into the dark night.

As soon as Violet's feet touched the ground, an arrow hit her arm.

"A spider jockey!" cried Leo.

Noah shot an arrow at the skeleton. Leo struck it with his sword while Violet and Katie focused on destroying the evil spider.

Despite being attacked by Noah and Leo, the skeleton was able to shoot arrows. One arrow hit Noah.

"I got it!" Leo called out as he hit the skeleton with his sword. The skeleton was destroyed. It dropped an arrow, which Leo picked up and placed in his inventory.

Violet was the one to destroy the spider. She used her sword and, with one hard smack, annihilated the spider. The spider dropped a spider eye, and Violet grabbed it for her inventory. She knew a spider eye was helpful when brewing potions.

Noah handed the group a potion to help them regain their energy. "We need to be strong. I know this isn't a long trip, but there are many hostile mobs lurking around these parts of the Overworld. We also need to be smart if we are going to survive."

The group took sips from the potion bottle. They were ready for anything that came their way. That is, until a silent killer crept up behind Noah.

Kaboom!

A creeper destroyed Noah as the gang watched.

Violet cried, "Oh no!" and she made her way back to the tree house. She wanted to be there when Noah respawned.

11
YOU'VE GOT A FRIEND

"**V**iolet," Noah called out as Violet stepped into the tree house.

Katie and Leo climbed up the ladder next. "There are a bunch of zombies approaching. What should we do?"

"Fight!" Noah led the gang down the ladder.

The zombies shuffled in the distance, and before long they approached the tree house.

Noah shot an arrow, which hit a zombie. This angered the beast and he lumbered toward Noah.

With their swords and bows and arrows out, Noah, Violet, Katie, and Leo battled the undead mob.

"Do you have any potions?" Violet asked the others. She was dismayed to see her inventory was empty.

"Yes," Katie took out a splash potion that was harmful to zombies and splashed them.

More zombies descended upon the group. Noah looked at the mob of zombies and expressed his fear, "I hope this battle doesn't destroy us."

"Even if it doesn't destroy us, it's going to set us back. We need to act fast. We have to save our friends." Violet was worried about the others, and what Daniel and Mac might be doing to them. She hoped they weren't on Hardcore mode.

"Violet!" a voice called out from the tree house.

Violet thought she was imagining it. She turned around and saw Hannah climbing down the ladder. Hannah was still wearing her rainbow skin.

"It's a rainbow griefer!" Katie shouted and aimed her arrow at Hannah.

"No—stop!" Noah ordered Katie. "It's Hannah!"

Violet questioned her, "How did you escape?"

"When they captured us, I had very little energy left. One yellow griefer threatened me and hit me with his diamond sword and I respawned in the tree house," explained Hannah.

"You need to change your skin," suggested Katie. "When the sun rises, the townspeople will attack you. We aren't fans of rainbow griefers here."

Hannah changed her skin while the others continued to battle the zombies. A couple of townspeople came out from their homes. They wore armor and helped the gang fight off the zombies.

One of the townspeople stood out from the others. He was an extremely skilled fighter and destroyed multiple zombies while the others were still battling a single zombie. When the battle was over, Noah introduced himself to the expert warrior.

"Who are you?" asked Noah.

"I'm Dash," the warrior replied.

"I'm Noah, and I want you to know I think you're an amazing fighter. I've never seen anyone battle zombies with that much skill."

Dash thanked him. He was blushing. Dash wasn't used to attention and replied, "I've had to battle a lot of zombies, so I've picked up some tricks."

"Why did you have to battle a lot of zombies?" asked Violet.

"They were always spawning on my farm," Dash told them. He explained that he was a wheat farmer and had lived in the town a long time, even when Daniel became the self-proclaimed leader of the town.

"You know Daniel has destroyed Supersonic, the new amusement park, right?" asked Katie.

"Yes, it's horrible. I wanted to ride the Dashing Coaster, but it was destroyed before I had the chance."

"We are going to rebuild the amusement park. You'll have a chance to ride the Dashing Coaster," Leo said quite passionately.

"But we need your help," Noah told Dash.

The sun began to rise as Dash asked, "How?"

"I've never seen anyone fight like you. We need you to help us beat Daniel. He has taken over a desert village," explained Noah. "We'd like you to come to the village and help us battle Daniel."

"He has also trapped our friends. He is planning something terrible—I just know it!" added Violet.

"Daniel destroyed my wheat farm. He made the rainbow griefers harvest my wheat and he kept me a prisoner. I would be more than happy to help you battle that evil guy," Dash told the group.

"Great!" Noah was happy Dash agreed to join them on their trip to the desert village.

"Should we go too?" asked Katie. She wasn't sure if she and Leo should stay behind and work on rebuilding the amusement park or battle Daniel.

"Yes, you should come too!" Violet told Katie. "When we defeat Daniel, we will all come back and rebuild Supersonic together."

"That's fantastic!" exclaimed Katie.

"Sounds like a plan!" added Leo.

"It's going to bigger and better than before," Violet reassured them. "Supersonic will be the most amazing amusement park in the Overworld."

"If we defeat Daniel, that is," Noah said. He knew Daniel was extremely powerful and defeating him wasn't going to be easy.

"We *will* defeat Daniel!" Violet corrected her friend Noah. She hoped what she said was true. She'd never admit her doubts about winning the battle, but she reminded herself they had defeated him in the past. Violet followed the others as they set out for the desert village. She imagined herself riding the Dashing Coaster and how it felt when the roller coaster went superfast.

When she was on the coaster, her heart beat faster and she felt invincible. She wanted to ride on the coaster again.

12
GREEDY GRIEFERS

The desert village was in sight when the gang was suddenly blasted with arrows.

"Where are they coming from?" Noah looked around but couldn't find anyone.

"It's too light out for skeletons to attack us." Violet also looked around. She could feel arrows strike her skin, but had no idea who was shooting at them.

"I think it's coming from behind that tree," Dash said as he ran through the dry grass in the Savanna Biome toward an acacia tree.

He found a horde of purple griefers clustered behind the tree. Dash splashed a potion on them and began to skillfully destroy the griefers. The others rushed to Dash's side, but he had already annihilated the majority of griefers. Noah struck the final griefer, just as a herd of white horses galloped across the savanna.

"We should tame them," suggested an excited Dash. "It's the fastest way to travel."

The group tamed the horses with Dash's help. They hopped on the horses and each rode one until they were able to access their horse's inventory. When the wild horses were calmed down, the gang each placed a saddle on their horse. Then they rode the tame animals toward the desert village.

"Get your bows and arrows out," ordered Noah as the gang approached the checkpoint.

Noah spotted Joe, who was also known as Redgriefer89.

"Aim and shoot!" Noah instructed. He took out his arrow and shot at Joe. Joe was surprised by the attack.

"Horses!" Joe shouted before he was destroyed.

Katie's arrow obliterated the orange griefer that stood next to Joe at the checkpoint. "Bull's-eye!"

The gang rode their white horses through the desert village filled with rainbow griefers, but nobody noticed these strangers on horseback. The sun was beginning to set, and the town was too busy heading into their homes for the night.

"This is good," Violet said to the others. "Nobody will notice that we aren't rainbow since it's getting dark."

"Should we build a place to stay?" asked Katie.

"No, we don't have time. We have to remain focused and find our friends," replied Noah.

"They need to be taken to the dungeon," a voice called out.

"Did you hear that?" asked Violet.

"Yes, where did it come from?" Noah replied.

"I don't know, but it sounds like Daniel." Violet turned her horse in the direction of the voice. "I think it's coming from that desert house."

"You're right!" Noah said as he heard the voice again.

Violet knew it was definitely Daniel's voice when she heard him say, "Once we bring them to the dungeon, we'll put them on Hardcore mode and destroy them!" Daniel's shrill laugh echoed throughout the village. The laugh was piercing, loud, and plain evil.

"He's just a one-trick pony," Noah said as he hopped off his horse and strode toward the house.

"What do you mean?" questioned Dash.

"When Daniel wants to destroy someone, he tries to put them on Hardcore mode. It's his only plan," remarked Noah.

"I know, you'd think he'd find another plan," Violet added as she also got off her horse and followed Noah.

The others dismounted and walked closely behind Noah.

"Do we have a plan?" questioned Violet.

"Our plan is to save our friends," replied Noah.

"That's not a plan. That's a goal," Violet retorted.

"It's just semantics," uttered Noah. He knew Violet was right, they needed a plan.

The gang stood by the door of the desert house. Two small cacti sat on either side of the entrance. Before they could enter, two red griefers attacked them.

"Gotcha!" one of the red griefers called out as he hit Violet with his sword.

Noah and his friends tried to fight back but the griefers threw a potion on the gang and it weakened them.

"We need to bring these evil folks to Daniel," the red griefer told his fellow evil griefer.

"No, we should keep them from Daniel," replied the other griefer.

"Why?" His friend seemed confused.

"They are worth something. These are the people Daniel told our entire village to look for, and we can use them to our advantage."

"You're so smart. We should totally do that," his red griefer friend replied.

The two griefers were so busy plotting how they could use the captives for their potential gain, they didn't notice Dash racing toward them with his diamond sword. Dash struck one of the red griefers, pushing him onto the cactus.

"Help!" the red griefer called out.

His friend couldn't help him because he, too, was thrown against the cactus. Katie had struck the other griefer with her sword and he fell onto the prickly plant.

The cacti damaged the griefers, but the gang finalized it when they struck the two griefers with their swords and destroyed them.

"See what happens when you get greedy," Noah said to his friends.

The gang could hear Daniel's voice call out, "I think I hear someone outside."

The door to the desert house opened. A flood of rainbow griefers sprinted from the home.

An orange griefer spotted Noah and shouted, "I found them! They're here!"

The gang fought with splash potions, arrows, and their enchanted diamond swords, but they were outnumbered. Even a skilled fighter like Dash was no match for the large griefer army.

Daniel walked out of the house ordering the griefer army, "Don't destroy them. Just capture them."

"We've got them!" a green griefer called to Daniel.

Daniel commended the group, "Good job, griefer army!"

The group was surrounded, and the rainbow griefers marched them into the house.

Daniel laughed, "I have big plans for you guys."

The gang walked into the house. One of the griefers asked Daniel, "What are your plans for them?"

Daniel replied, "Don't ask questions. You just take orders."

The griefer army led the group down the stairs into a dark room with a couple of torches providing a dull light to the musty basement. Noah spotted Hannah in the distance. She was in a jail cell, trapped behind bars.

"Help!" she cried.

Noah wanted to help, but he knew, for now, he was helpless.

13
DÉJÀ VU

"Look at you guys. You should be happy that you've been reunited," Daniel cackled as he slammed the door of the jail behind them.

"We're going to get out. We're going to be free," Violet shouted at Daniel.

"I'm having a feeling of déjà vu." Daniel smiled. "I've heard that before, and guess what: I always come back and get my way. I am going to win. You might as well just give up."

"Never!" shouted Violet.

"And we will rebuild Supersonic," Katie blurted out.

"How funny," Daniel put his hand on the prison bars, "you're worried about an amusement park, when you should be worried about yourselves. This is the end, my friends."

The gang all began to shout at once, but Daniel didn't listen. He just removed the torches and walked up the stairs with his griefer army, leaving the gang trapped in a pitch-dark basement.

"What are we going to do?" Will asked them. He was terrified.

"We're going to escape," Violet replied. She paced around the small cell. Her friends looked at her, hoping she had a plan.

"Watch out!" Ben called to his friends as a spider crawled through the prison cell.

Noah grabbed his diamond sword from his inventory and struck the spider. Violet watched Noah destroy the spider and said, "I know how we are going to escape!"

"How?" the group asked in unison.

Violet paced as she spoke. "I mean, for all of his planning, Daniel never pays attention to the most important detail."

"What?" the group asked.

"Daniel never emptied our inventories," Violet said. "We aren't trapped. We have weapons . . . and that means we still have power."

"Yes!" Noah called out. "We have pickaxes!"

The group took pickaxes from their inventories and began to dig into the ground.

"Watch out for lava," Violet warned as they dug their pickaxes deep into the ground.

They worked hard together until they had a deep a hole. Noah said, "We need to climb in."

One by one they each jumped into the hole. Ben suggested, "I think we should light a torch and place it down here."

Hannah took a torch from her inventory and placed it on the wall of their makeshift cave.

"We need to dig a seriously deep tunnel next," Noah instructed the group. "When we begin to dig an exit hole out of the tunnel, we want to be so far from this desert house that we have a chance to escape."

"But how are we going to defeat Daniel?" questioned Violet.

"We just need to get out of here first," replied Noah.

"I think I see something blue," Marco told the group as he dug the tunnel.

"Wow, I didn't think we were deep enough to find diamonds!" marveled Hannah.

Violet walked over to Marco. "You're right. You did find diamonds. How amazing!"

The gang began to grab the diamonds and place them in their inventories.

"They are going to come in very handy," said Leo. "We'll need all these resources when we rebuild Supersonic."

The group used their pickaxes and worked hard. Violet looked back. "We've dug a fairly long tunnel. I wonder if we should start thinking about digging upward and getting out of here."

"Let's just dig a bit more. I want to make sure we are far enough from Daniel's headquarters."

Hannah paused. "Oh no," she cried out.

"What is it?" asked Ben.

"Shh!" Hannah told the group, "I think I hear voices."

Everyone stood silently until Violet whispered, "You're right! We aren't alone."

Noah spotted rainbow griefers behind them. "They found us! Dig up!"

The group furiously dug a hole into the top of the tunnel. Noah was the first to climb out. He called to the others, "Be prepared for battle!"

As each of them scrambled out of the tunnel, they were surprised to see a horde of skeletons shooting arrows at them.

"I thought we were going to battle rainbow griefers," Violet said as she tried to fight the skeletons.

Dash struck four skeletons and destroyed them.

"This guy can fight!" exclaimed Ben as he dodged an arrow flying in his direction.

"I know," Noah said proudly of his friend Dash. "He is the best fighter. We're in good hands."

As the gang battled the skeletons, the rainbow griefers emerged from the tunnel and shot arrows at them.

Dash charged at the griefers, striking them skillfully with his sword. Within seconds he wiped out the entire batch of rainbow griefers trailing them.

"Good job," praised Noah.

"I'm not finished yet," Dash replied breathlessly as he raced toward the remaining skeletons and obliterated them.

The sun began to rise. Violet looked around and realized they were in the middle of the desert village.

"Everyone is waking up," Violet told them. "We have to get out of here!"

The gang hurried toward home. They knew the next time they battled Daniel, it would be on their turf.

They raced past the empty checkpoint. Violet was hoping they'd find another herd of horses as they made their way through the Savanna Biome, but there weren't any horses roaming around the grassy land.

"What are we going to do when we get back to our village?" asked Hannah.

"Don't worry," Violet announced, "I have a great plan."

14

RETURNING THE FAVOR

The first person the gang spotted as they entered their village was Valentino the Butcher.

"You're back!" Valentino called out to his friends.

"How's everything in town?" asked Noah.

"It's been quiet," replied Valentino.

"That's because we were busy fighting Daniel in the Desert Biome," said Noah.

Valentino asked, "Did you defeat that evil villain?"

Noah looked at the ground; he was embarrassed to admit they had fled the town without destroying Daniel and his minions. "No, we didn't."

"Oh no. Does that mean Daniel is coming back here?"

"Yes," said Violet, "but we'll be prepared. We are going to defeat Daniel."

"And we're going to rebuild Supersonic," added Leo.

"In fact, we should get started on rebuilding the amusement park right away," Violet told the gang.

"Seriously?" questioned Hannah. "That's what you want us to work on? I mean, shouldn't we spend our time brainstorming a plan to defeat Daniel?"

"Trust me"—Violet smiled—"this is a part of the plan."

Valentino said, "Great! Go rebuild the amusement park. I can't wait to work at my restaurant again. I loved working at the park. It was so festive."

"It will be festive again. Daniel isn't going to stop our happiness," said Katie.

The group was in a jovial mood. They were excited to hear Violet's plan, but once they reached the park's entrance, their mood became quite somber.

"This is a lot worse than I imagined," Violet said as she stared at the ruined park, now flooded with lava.

"I told you all that Daniel flooded the park." Leo shook his head at the mess that flowed through the park.

"How are we going to rid the park of lava and rebuild?" Violet worried that her plan might not work out.

"Should we rebuild the park in another spot?" suggested Will.

"No, there isn't another spot," replied Katie. "And we can't just leave this park covered in lava. It's a symbol of defeat."

Everyone agreed with Katie. They must clean up the park and rebuild the amusement park on the same land.

"Do you need help?" a voice called out.

Violet and the gang turned around and were surprised to see the entire town standing behind them.

One of the townspeople said, "You're not alone. We can help clean up the park."

On further inspection, Violet realized the entire town was carrying buckets.

"We'd love your help." Violet beamed in relief.

Using one bucket at a time, the townspeople emptied the toxic substance from the amusement park. It took an entire village and an entire day to rid the park of lava, but as night began to set in, the park was clean.

"Now we just have to rebuild," said Violet. She thanked the townspeople, "Without your help this park could not be rebuilt. You are all warriors in the battle against Daniel."

One of the townspeople spoke, "As you might recall, many of us were forced into being a part of Daniel's rainbow griefer army. We will do anything to see him defeated."

The townspeople cheered. Violet never felt happier. Even though their situation was dire and rebuilding the park wouldn't be an easy job, she was happy to see that so many people wanted to help.

"You are the strongest asset we have in this battle against Daniel. Knowing that we have your assistance will help us ultimately defeat Daniel."

The townspeople cheered, until one cried out, "I've been hit!"

Skeletons descended upon the town.

"More skeletons!" shouted Marco.

"I don't think it's a coincidence that we keep seeing skeletons. I'm sure Daniel is summoning them," noted Violet as she shot an arrow at the bony beasts clanging through her dimly lit town.

The gang and the townspeople battled the skeletons. Violet was upset that many townspeople were destroyed by the bony terrors.

Click! Clack! Clang! More skeletons paraded through the town.

"Do you think he has a skeleton spawner outside the town?" questioned Noah, as he struck a skeleton with his diamond sword.

"Should we search for it?" asked Ben.

"It may be our only option," replied Noah.

Noah and Ben made their way through the battleground and walked outside of the village.

"They're coming from over this hill," Ben pointed out.

Noah and Ben hiked over the hill and spotted a cave. "It must be in there!" The duo cautiously entered the cave. Noah quickly found a cave spider and destroyed it.

"I see it!" Ben called out.

Noah and Ben took out torches and placed them by the skeleton spawner.

"Thankfully the skeleton invasion is over." Noah smiled.

"For now." Ben wasn't convinced the skeletons were really gone. Daniel was tricky. He might have another spawner close by.

Noah and Ben were emerging from the cave when Noah suddenly shouted, "Watch out!"

It was too late. The creeper exploded and Ben was destroyed.

Noah knew Ben would respawn in the desert village. He didn't know if he should head to the desert village alone and protect Ben or if he should go back to the town and get help. As he stood in the darkness, he felt very conflicted about the decision. He was so immersed in thought that he didn't notice a green creeper silently sidle up to him.

Kaboom! Noah was destroyed. He respawned in the tree house. The gang was climbing up the ladder when they saw Noah.

"Where's Ben?" Hannah asked him.

"We were both destroyed by creepers," replied Noah.

"Oh no!" Hannah gasped. "We need to go and save him."

"We can't. We need to sleep first." Violet didn't want to appear heartless, but she knew the gang needed to sleep in the tree house. If they didn't, some of them would respawn in the Desert Biome.

"But you don't realize where Daniel had us sleep. It was a horrible place. He is such a bad person. We were sleeping in a dirty cave before he placed us in that cell," Hannah said as she walked toward the ladder.

"We need to sleep here and find Ben in the morning. If not, and if you are destroyed during a battle, you will respawn in the desert."

Hannah paused. She knew Violet was right, but she wouldn't be able to sleep with Ben in danger. "But Ben—"

Noah interrupted, "Ben is a strong person. He'll be fine."

Hannah didn't know if that was true, but she was tired. She climbed into her bed, and within seconds everyone was asleep.

15
GRAND REOPENING

"**G**ood morning!" Ben called out as the sun began to rise.

"Ben!" Hannah was so happy to see her friend standing in the tree house. "How did you escape?"

"The village was empty," Ben told them.

"Empty?" Violet was surprised to hear that.

"I have no idea where everyone went, but there aren't any people in the desert village anymore," said Ben.

"Daniel must have relocated his group," said Noah.

Violet paced the length of the tree house. "I don't like this at all. I have a feeling we are in for a serious attack today."

"But we must rebuild the park," said Katie.

"Yes, we will rebuild the park today," Violet reassured her friend. "I'm sure once we announce a grand reopening, Daniel will stage his attack."

"You're right," confirmed Noah. "Daniel loves an audience. As soon as the park is filled with people from all over the Overworld, he will have a big audience for his attack."

"Let's go and rebuild!" announced Violet.

"But I don't want the park to be destroyed." Leo was worried about the park. He didn't want to rebuild and have the park simply demolished again. He thought that was pointless.

"Once we stage the grand reopening, we'll be ready for Daniel. If we're properly prepared, we will defeat him," said Violet.

"And if we have the entire town ready to battle along with us, there is no way he can win," added Hannah.

Violet handed out cake to everyone. "We must eat. We need our strength. Today is going to be a victorious day."

After they finished eating, the group exited the tree house and walked to Supersonic.

"Wow!" exclaimed Katie as she stared at the large crowd standing in front of the park ready to help out.

"We told you we'd help you rebuild," a townsperson called to the gang.

Katie and Leo stood on a block. Katie spoke to the crowd, "Thank you for assisting us. You have no idea how much this means to us. We couldn't rebuild without your aid. You are truly the best townspeople ever."

The townspeople cheered.

Leo said, "We have the construction plans for the park. We will break up into teams and everyone will help rebuild a ride. I think we have enough people to rebuild the entire park quite quickly."

Leo and Katie divided the townspeople into groups, and each group gathered in the area where they were rebuilding a ride.

Violet worked on reconstructing the food court. Noah and the others were put on the most important project at the park—rebuilding the Dashing Coaster.

Violet stood by the food court and called out to Noah, "When you're done with the coaster, I want to be one of the first to ride it!"

Everyone worked together on the rides, and there was a bustling jovial energy throughout the park. Katie and Leo were hopeful the park would be finished within a few days.

Katie reminded Violet, "We need to start planning the festivities for the grand reopening."

"Yes, we will announce the grand reopening to the Overworld so Daniel will hear about it. Once we do that, we can begin staging our attack on Daniel," Violet replied as she constructed the walls of the food court.

Valentino stood beside Violet. "I'm excited to start cooking again. You did a great job with my restaurant."

They were making progress until it started to rain.

"Maybe we don't have to wait for the grand reopening for Daniel to attack us," Violet said with a frown. She was upset.

"This rain can just be a natural occurrence in the Overworld," said Katie.

"Doubtful," Violet replied, as an arrow from a skeleton struck her arm.

"But skeletons usually spawn in the rain." Katie didn't want to believe Daniel was attacking them.

"Yes, that's true." Violet grabbed her sword. "But look at how many skeletons have spawned. There are hundreds. Now that's not normal."

Katie had to agree with Violet—this must be apart of Daniel's plan.

"Everyone, we must all battle this skeleton army," Noah directed the townspeople who were helping rebuild Supersonic.

Arrows flew through the air. As skeletons collapsed, the townspeople grabbed whatever the skeletons dropped on the ground. They picked up bones, arrows, and other items and placed them in their inventories.

Dash was valiantly battling a large group of skeletons when the sun began to shine.

"Thankfully!" exclaimed Dash.

"Really? You're glad the battle is over?" Noah was surprised; he assumed Dash loved battling the bony beasts.

"Yes. Just because I am a skilled fighter, that doesn't mean it's easy for me. Each battle takes a lot out of me," confessed Dash.

Leo hurried past Noah and Dash. He held a megaphone and shouted, "Everyone, we have to get back to work. The grand reopening is taking place very soon!"

Noah and Dash joined the others. They were excited to finish working on Supersonic. They had to admit they were both looking forward to riding the Dashing Coaster.

There weren't any interruptions from Daniel, so the gang was able to work steadily on the park. Leo walked around the park and inspected the various rides. He stood on a podium and made an announcement: "The park is completed!"

Everyone cheered.

"We will hold the grand reopening tomorrow!" announced Katie.

"But to celebrate the completion, we are allowing everyone who helped us to take a free ride on all the attractions," Leo told the crowd.

The crowd cheered again and quickly lined up for the rides. Violet and Noah were among the first people on line for the Dashing Coaster.

Violet sat next to Noah on the ride. She let out a scream when they went down the first big hill. Violet was having the best time of her life, but she worried that tomorrow she'd have to battle Daniel at the grand reopening. For now, she tried to stop thinking about Daniel. The coaster cars clattered to a stop at the end of the ride.

Noah asked, "Want to go for a second ride?"

"Yes!" replied Violet. Today she was going to have fun.

16
CREEPERS!

The gang woke up early and looked out the window of the tree house.

Katie let out a sigh of relief. "It looks like Supersonic is still there."

"We didn't hear any explosions last night," Leo said. He walked to the window and stood beside Katie. "So I knew it would be okay."

The gang hurried down the ladder and headed to Supersonic. They were excited for the grand reopening.

"Wow, look at how many people are already lined up to get into the park!" Katie was excited.

Crowds of people stood outside the gate. Violet looked for rainbow griefers that might be hiding around the amusement park.

"It looks like we are safe," Violet said, but she spoke too soon, as a silent army was creeping toward the park.

"Creepers!" Noah screamed. Over a hundred creepers silently moved toward the park entrance. They exploded.

Kaboom!

The intense creeper explosion destroyed everyone at the park entrance. Violet and the gang stared in disbelief as the happy group exploded.

"That had to be Daniel." Violet was furious.

"I've never seen that many creepers at once. And the explosion they set off was so powerful!" Trent was devastated.

"I can't imagine what else he has planned," Marco said, and he thought about all the people from his town that were now a part of Daniel's rainbow griefer army.

"Look!" Noah shouted.

A group of rainbow griefers marched toward them. The griefers held bows and arrows. They halted and began to shoot at the gang.

"Stop!" Noah shouted, but the griefers didn't listen to him and continued to shoot arrows.

"Where's Daniel?" Violet called out to the griefers as she shot arrows and also dodged them. There was no reply.

"Looking for me?" Daniel laughed as he walked into the thick of battle with his enchanted diamond armor.

"Stop this!" demanded Violet.

"Why should I?" he laughed again.

Mac walked toward the park; trailing behind him was an all-blue griefer army carrying diamond swords. The blue griefers sprinted toward the group and began to hit them.

Violet was destroyed. She respawned in the tree house. It was empty. Again, she was the first person to respawn. She felt as if she were failing her friends and that her fighting skills weren't as strong as the others'.

Ben respawned in the house next. He looked over at Violet. "Daniel summoned the Ender Dragon again. Now it's going to fly into the rides and destroy the park. He is back to his old tricks."

Then Hannah respawned in her bed. "The Ender Dragon . . ." Hannah rushed the words out and dashed to the window.

Violet and Ben followed behind her.

"I don't see it," said Violet. She couldn't spot the Ender Dragon.

"We have to find out what happened," Ben said and he climbed down the ladder. The gang raced to the park.

Leo rushed over to meet them. "Katie destroyed the Ender Dragon!"

Violet, Ben, and Hannah didn't have time to congratulate her because they spotted Daniel and Mac. The evil duo pointed their swords at Noah and Dash.

Ben shot an arrow and hit Daniel. He was destroyed. "Wow!" Ben was amazed at his quick success.

Hannah shot an arrow that destroyed Mac. "Is this luck or is this a trick?" wondered Hannah.

Once their leaders were destroyed, the rainbow griefers began to attack the group. Arrows flew through the sky until Marco jumped onto the podium and shouted, "Who remembers me? I am Marco and I lived in the desert village."

Surprisingly, the rainbow griefers stopped shooting their bows and arrows and listened to Marco.

"I was sent here to destroy this park, but I couldn't do it. When I saw the cotton candy and the rides, I just wanted to go on them. I didn't want to hurt anyone. I wanted to have fun. This park is amazing. There is a roller coaster that is superfast, and a Ferris wheel that's so large I can see our hometown from the top of it," Marco informed them.

The rainbow griefers listened. One of the blue griefers changed his skin back to his old skin and said, "Marco, remember me?"

Marco walked over to his old friend. "Yes, of course I remember you, Doug."

The other rainbow griefers watched as Doug joined Marco on the podium.

Doug said, "It's okay. Change back to your old skin. Get rid of the rainbow skin Daniel forced you to wear. Start using your old names. No longer will Daniel use a color and a number to refer to us. We are individuals. We have identities."

Marco added, "We have to stay strong. Once we defeat Daniel, we can go back to our desert village and live a peaceful life."

The rainbow griefers began to change into their old skins. A small group of orange griefers remained orange. Instead of changing their skins, they shot arrows at the group.

Dash and Noah raced toward the orange griefers and attacked them. With a few hits, the orange griefers were destroyed.

"Daniel has lost his griefer army again!" declared Noah.

The group cheered. The crowds returned to the park entrance. The ticket booths opened and folks lined up.

Violet watched the crowd lining up for the Dashing Coaster. She was pleased they had defeated the rainbow griefers and the park was open, but she knew they still had to defeat Daniel. She realized the battle wasn't over.

"Violet," Noah called out. "Do you want to ride the log flume?"

"No," replied Violet. "I think we should go on the Ferris wheel. We can have a good view of the entire area and maybe we will spot Daniel."

"Do you still think he's going to stage something now that we've destroyed his rainbow griefer army?" Noah truly believed the battle was over.

"I don't trust Daniel," Violet replied as she headed for the Ferris wheel.

Noah and Violet climbed into the Ferris wheel's car. They rode around a couple of times before they stopped at the top.

"I can see the desert village," said Violet.

"Do you see Daniel? Or Mac?" Noah tried to spot the evil duo.

Violet looked out of the car but didn't see them anywhere. She let out a sigh of relief. She was going to enjoy the ride. When they exited the Ferris wheel, she spotted Mac by the Dashing Coaster. He was carrying a brick of TNT.

17

A WILD RIDE

Violet ran toward Mac as Noah shot arrows at him. She struck Mac with her diamond sword.

"Give me that TNT!" demanded Violet.

"Game over!" shouted Noah as he put his bow and arrow away and took out his enchanted diamond sword.

Mac laughed, "It's too late. We're going to blow this park to smithereens."

"Never!" Violet struck Mac again with her sword.

Dash and Trent raced over to help Noah and Violet.

"We have Daniel!" Dash called out.

Trent clarified, "We trapped Daniel!"

Mac couldn't believe his ears. "What? Impossible!"

Violet struck Mac again, but Noah told her to stop. "We don't want to destroy Mac. If we do, he'll respawn somewhere else."

"Why don't you just put me on Hardcore mode and destroy me forever?" Mac taunted them.

"No, that's the way Daniel operates—we don't do things like that," replied Violet.

Trent stood in front of Mac. "You're coming with me. You're going to be reunited with your evil friend."

Trent and Dash led the way, as Noah and Violet walked behind them with Mac. They pointed their diamond swords at Mac so he couldn't escape.

Daniel was trapped in a small jail cell in the amusement park's security office.

"You're not going to get away with this," Daniel protested.

"Looks like we already have," Noah said as he glared at Daniel.

Dash opened the jail cell and led Mac into the cell. "Now, both of you empty your inventories."

"No way!" declared Mac.

Even Mac was shocked when Daniel handed over all the loot and resources from his inventory. "You won," Daniel muttered.

Mac followed Daniel and gave them everything from his inventory.

Violet wondered what Daniel was planning. This was too easy. She wondered if this might be a distraction that Daniel was staging. Maybe he had other people working for him and they were going to ignite the TNT and blow up the park. She stood by the bars at the jail cell and demanded, "Tell me where you placed the TNT and who is going to activate it!"

"What are you talking about?" Daniel looked at Violet.

"I don't trust you, Daniel. You're too sneaky to get caught," Violet told him.

"Maybe I messed up and that's why I was caught. Why don't you trust me?" Daniel let out a chuckle.

"Gang," Violet called to her friends, "check this park for TNT."

Noah organized a group to check every inch of Supersonic for TNT. Violet and Ben stayed behind to guard Daniel.

"You're not going to find anything," Daniel said with a smile.

But Daniel's smile quickly turned to a frown when Noah marched into the amusement park's security office with three orange griefers.

"I found them hiding by the rides with bricks of TNT," Noah informed Daniel.

Dash entered the security office. "There is no more TNT in the park. We have taken it all to a secure location."

"Excellent work!" Violet commended her friend and then said to Daniel, "I knew you were planning something."

Noah placed the orange griefers behind bars with Daniel and Mac.

18
FUN HOUSE

Violet was excited to finally enjoy the amusement park. Now that Daniel and Mac were behind bars, she knew everyone was safe.

"Let's go on the Dashing Coaster!" Hannah said to Violet.

They jogged to the roller coaster. When the people buying tickets saw them approach the ride, they waved them to the front of the line.

"No, we can wait. We don't need special treatment," Violet protested.

"But you saved the park," said one of the people on the line.

"Yes, but that doesn't mean we get to cut the line. Thanks for offering, though!" Violet was simply happy waiting with her friend Hannah.

Noah walked over to them. He was eating a sandwich.

"Where did you get that food? It looks so yummy." Hannah eyed Noah's sandwich.

"I got it from Valentino's shop." Noah took a bite.

"We need to go there after we ride the Dashing Coaster." Violet looked at Noah and advised, "I think you should wait a bit before you go on this ride."

Noah was perplexed. "Why?"

"You need to digest your food first," replied Violet.

Noah smiled. "I guess you're right. I think I'll stick to the Ferris wheel."

"We'll go on the Ferris wheel with you," said Violet.

Hannah agreed. "Let's go on the Ferris wheel first. We can ride the Dashing Coaster when the line is shorter."

The gang walked to the Ferris wheel. On the way over to the ride, Violet spotted Marco. He was walking with Doug.

"Hi, we've been looking for you. We want to thank you for all your help, and to tell you that we're going back to our desert village."

The gang was sad to see them go, but they knew the desert village wasn't very far away and they could visit.

Will and Trent also joined them, and Will announced, "We're leaving too."

"Wow, everyone is leaving us." Violet was sad.

"We are going to join our treasure-hunting friends, Henry, Max, and Lucy, to search for treasure under the sea in an ocean monument."

"Sounds like fun!" exclaimed Noah.

"Do you want to go on one last Ferris wheel ride with us?" asked Hannah.

The gang climbed aboard the Ferris wheel cars. Violet looked out from the top and was glad she didn't have to search for Daniel, Mac, or any rainbow griefers lurking in the landscape. When they hopped off the Ferris wheel, Noah suggested they take a stroll through the Fun House.

"I've never been in a Fun House before," confessed Marco.

"Me neither," said Violet.

The gang entered the Fun House and walked through a room filled with various mirrors. Some of the mirrors made them look small and others made them look tall.

"You look funny!" Hannah blurted out as she looked at Violet's elongated body in the mirror.

"I guess that's why they call it a Fun House!" Violet exclaimed.

The gang began to laugh heartily as they looked at each other in the mirrors' reflections. Without having to worry about Daniel, they were finally free to have fun again. The grand reopening of Supersonic was a success!

THE END